Maisy Goes to Work
Sticker Book

Lucy Cousins

Take the sticker pages out of the middle of this book.
Open the pages so the stickers and the pictures
in the book can be seen side by side.
Read the words on each page.
Children can choose which sticker to peel off
and where to put it in each picture.

WALKER BOOKS
AND SUBSIDIARIES
LONDON • BOSTON • SYDNEY • AUCKLAND

Farmer Maisy is feeding the lambs.

Who is feeding
the chickens?

Find Doctor Eddie's bag.

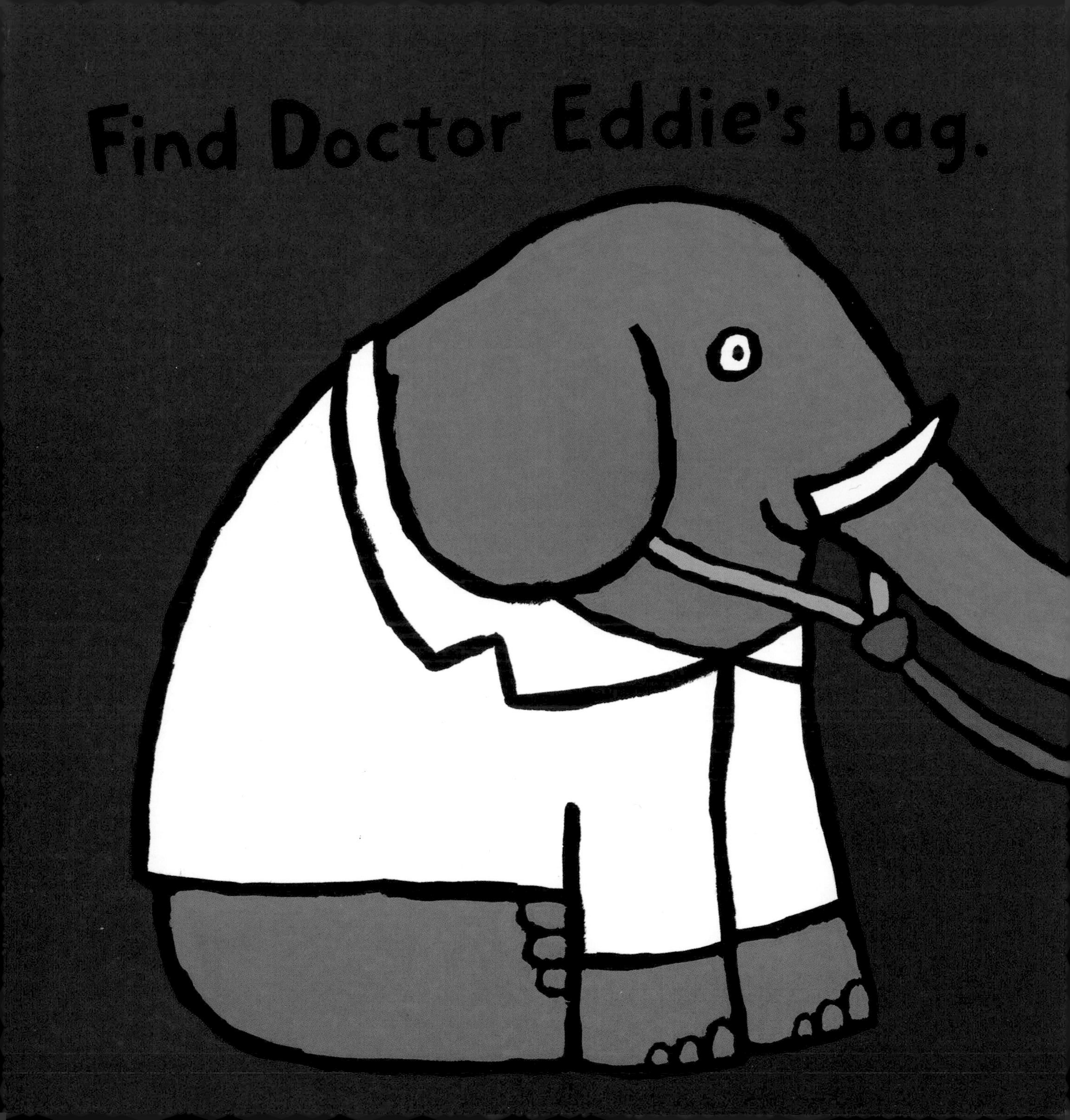

Dress Nurse Tallulah.
Who is feeling poorly?

Cyril needs his hat and apron.

Charley needs more cakes!

Maisy is diving. Put on
her goggles and flippers.

Can you find the treasure?

Where are
Charley's hat
and boots?
What does
he catch?

Dress Cyril in his firefighter's uniform.

Who is stuck in the tree? How will Cyril rescue her?

Maisy is flying!
Put her
scarf on.